Are tomatoes vegetables or fruit?

Written by Catherine Baker

Illustrated by Nathalie Ortega

Collins

What's in this book?

Listen and say

tomato

seeds

Download the audio at www.collins.co.uk/839669

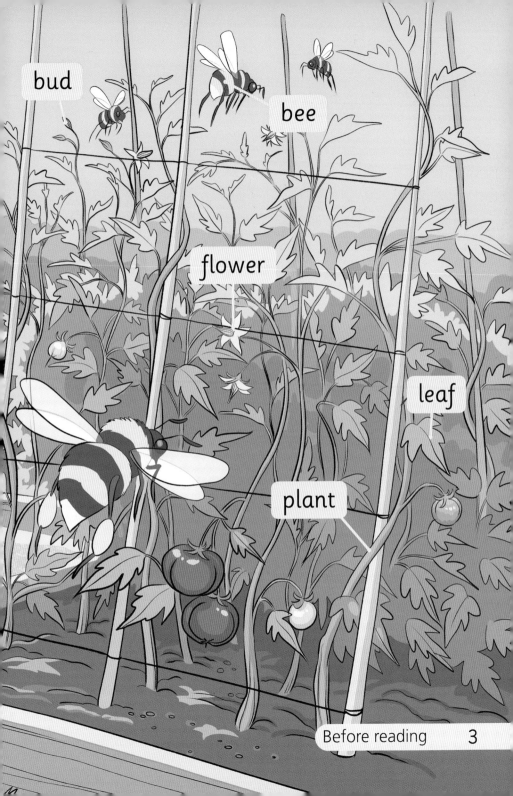

bud

bee

flower

leaf

plant

Jaya and her mum are at the market. "Look!" says Jaya. "The tomatoes are with the fruit *and* with the vegetables."

Both are correct!

tomatoes

vegetables

Vegetables are plants.
Food with vegetables isn't sweet. We eat
tomatoes in soups, salads and pies.
This food isn't sweet. We do not eat
tomato cake or tomato ice cream!

A fruit is a part of a plant. The fruit has the plant's seeds.

Plants need seeds to grow. The seeds fall on the ground and start to grow.

seed

After many days, new plants grow from the seeds.

Cut open a tomato. What's inside?

There is a lot of juice. There are lots of seeds, too!

The seeds show us that a tomato is a fruit.

tomato

The seeds of the tomato plant grow inside the tomato. New tomato plants can grow from these seeds.

How do tomato plants grow?

1 Some tomato seeds fall on the ground.

2 The seeds get water from the rain.

3 The seeds start growing.

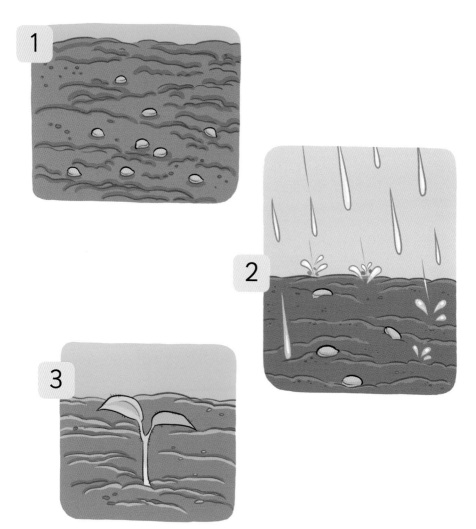

4 A small plant starts growing. Its leaves are very small.

5 The plant gets bigger and bigger. More and more leaves grow.

6 Flower buds start growing on the young tomato plant.

7 The buds open in the hot sun. The flowers are yellow. Bees fly up to the flowers.

8 The bees take pollen from the flowers. They carry the pollen from flower to flower. The pollen makes the fruit grow.

pollen

Small green tomatoes
start growing. The tomatoes are
the fruit of the tomato plant.

The tomatoes grow bigger and bigger
in the hot sun.

They need a lot of water, too!

After many days, the tomatoes are orange.
The tomatoes grow bigger and bigger.

Now they are big red tomatoes!

Look inside the big red tomatoes.
What can you see?

Yes – lots of seeds. You can plant these
seeds, and start again!

More tomato plants will grow from the seeds. These tomato plants will grow fruit, too.

Tomatoes are fruit *and* vegetables!
They have seeds, and that means
they are fruit.

We eat them in food that isn't sweet, and
that means they are vegetables.

These foods are vegetables and fruit, too!

cucumber

pumpkin

pepper

You can find tomatoes in lots of fantastic foods. Which of these is your favourite?

tomato salad

tomato soup

tomato sauce

pizza

21

Picture dictionary

Listen and repeat

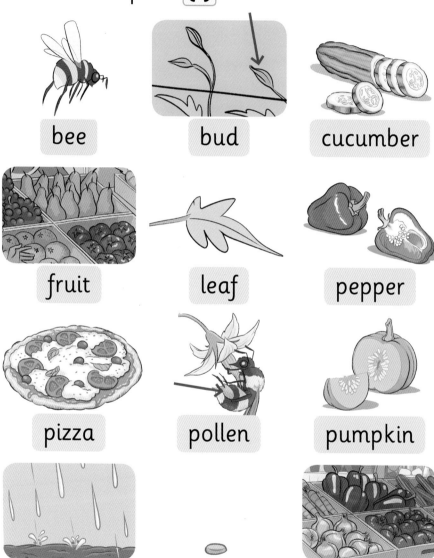

bee

bud

cucumber

fruit

leaf

pepper

pizza

pollen

pumpkin

rain

seed

vegetables

1 Look and order

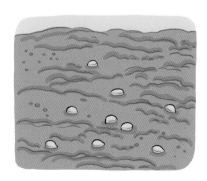

2 Listen and say

Collins

Published by Collins
An imprint of HarperCollins*Publishers*
Westerhill Road
Bishopbriggs
Glasgow
G64 2QT

HarperCollins*Publishers*
1st Floor, Watermarque Building
Ringsend Road
Dublin 4
Ireland

William Collins' dream of knowledge for all began with the publication of his first book in 1819.

A self-educated mill worker, he not only enriched millions of lives, but also founded a flourishing publishing house. Today, staying true to this spirit, Collins books are packed with inspiration, innovation and practical expertise. They place you at the centre of a world of possibility and give you exactly what you need to explore it.

© HarperCollins*Publishers* Limited 2020

10 9 8 7 6 5 4 3 2

ISBN 978-0-00-839669-5

Collins® and COBUILD® are registered trademarks of HarperCollins*Publishers* Limited

www.collins.co.uk/elt

Author: Catherine Baker
Illustrator: Nathalie Ortega (Beehive)
Series editor: Rebecca Adlard
Commissioning editor: Zoë Clarke
Publishing manager: Lisa Todd
Product managers: Jennifer Hall and Caroline Green
In-house editor: Alma Puts Keren
Project manager: Emily Hooton
Editor: Frances Amrani
Proofreaders: Natalie Murray and Michael Lamb
Cover designer: Kevin Robbins
Typesetter: 2Hoots Publishing Services Ltd
Audio produced by id audio, London
Reading guide author: Emma Wilkinson
Production controller: Rachel Weaver
Printed and bound by: GPS Group, Slovenia

Download the audio for this book and a reading guide for parents and teachers at www.collins.co.uk/839669